Cover and interior illustration by Zuzana Svobodová
Book design by Peggy Collins, Bookery Design Shop
Author's photograph by Aliyah Dastour

Hardcover: 978-1-7336109-2-6

Library of Congress Control Number: 2019913836

The Easter Bunny mysteriously shares a crazy adventure with two other holiday icons in this humorous tale celebrating cooperation and teamwork.

Printed and bound in the United States of America

First Edition

SWEETBEET BOOKS

The ~~Easter~~ Christmas Bunny's Wild Adventure

by Alma Hammond

illustrated by Zuzana Svobodová

Glad greetings, everyone.
Let me tell you some rhymes
about the Easter Bunny's
adventures across
seasonal times.

A week before Easter,
the Easter Bunny
was practicing his skills,
carrying baskets of eggs
over paths, bridges,
and hills.

There was Easter
egg painting,
hiding,
and stacking,
until not
a single
Easter Bunny
talent was
lacking!

Out of all the rest,
he loved hopping the best.
Hopping so high,
he flew up to the sky.

He rocketed through
time and space
at an out-of-this-world
lightning-speed pace!

Making winged creatures
duck and cover,
the Easter Bunny
bounced off to discover...

With a thump
and a whoosh,
he just couldn't believe,
he landed amid
the town's cold
Christmas Eve.

The Easter Bunny soared
through a whole other holiday,
buckled up next to Santa
in his shiny, red sleigh!

"Ho, ho, ho," bellowed Santa.
"I'm late delivering presents, and you are just the one to hop down the chimneys and get the job done."

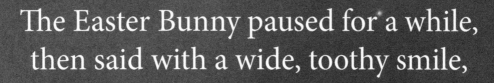

The Easter Bunny paused for a while,
then said with a wide, toothy smile,

"Why, Santa,
I'm flattered you'd ask!"
"I won't let you down,
I'm up to the task."

The Easter Bunny
grabbed the big bag of toys
to deliver the presents
to good girls and boys.

Hopping on roofs,
down the chimneys he went,
learning what being Santa
at Christmas time meant.

With the last present under the tree,

the magic of Christmas,
the Easter Bunny could see.

Then with a giant hop,
back to Easter he went
to find a bright green assistant,
who was heaven sent.

If the Easter Bunny could help
on a Christmas Eve run,
why couldn't St. Patrick's leprechaun help
him get Easter things done?

"Top o' the morn!
Your planning has slowed!
Ye are running late.
I'll help lighten your load!"

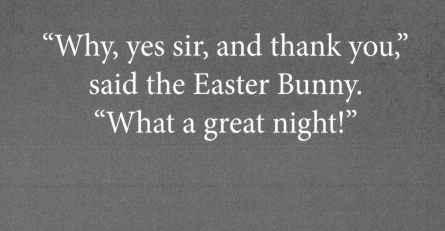

"Why, yes sir, and thank you,"
said the Easter Bunny.
"What a great night!"

They went delivering eggs
before Easter's first light.

Yes, working together is quicker.
Two is better than one.
Plus having a partner is a whole lot more fun!

Alma Hammond

Alma Hammond is the award-winning author of picture books that are inspired by her love of nature and travel, and that promote good self-esteem. For other books by Alma Hammond, go to www.sweetbeetbooks.com. Alma lives with her husband, Bob, her dog, Stazi, and her two cats, Violet and Daisy, in Bethesda, MD. When she isn't writing, Alma enjoys doing yoga, cooking, and traveling.

Zuzana Svobodová

Illustrator Zuzana Svobodová uses both digital and traditional techniques, as well as the world of fantasy delivered happily by her own children, to bring stories to life. Zuzana lives with her husband, Roman, and her two children, Lucia and Jakub, in Slovakia. When she isn't working on illustrations, Zuzana enjoys drawing, dreaming, teaching yoga, drinking coffee, and baking sweets.

Circle your favorite character in the book

Why do you like this character best?

Draw a line connecting each character with its holiday

St. Patrick's Day   Christmas   Easter

Which holiday do you like best?

Why do you like this holiday best?

Lightning Source UK Ltd.
Milton Keynes UK
UKHW051833121019
351432UK00005B/108/P